Danger Ahead!

A Tonka Joe® Adventure

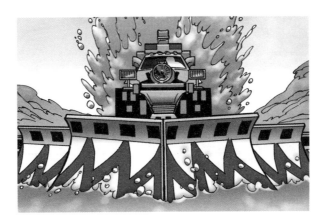

by Justine and Ron Fontes
Illustrated by Redondo/Mitchell

ISBN 0-439-25910-X

TONKA® and TONKA JOE® are trademarks of Hasbro, Inc.
Used with permission.
Copyright © 2001 Hasbro, Inc.
All rights reserved. Published by Scholastic, Inc.
SCHOLASTIC, CARTWHEEL BOOKS, and associated logos are trademarks and/or registered trademarks of Scholastic Inc.

10 9 8 7 6 5 4 3
Printed in the U.S.A.
First printing, May 2001

02 03 04 05
40

Cartwheel
B·O·O·K·S®

SCHOLASTIC INC.

New York   Toronto   London   Auckland   Sydney   Mexico City   New Delhi   Hong Kong

Flames roared through the shattered windows of Fred's Fireworks Factory! The firemen fighting the raging flames didn't know how the fire had started. But they were sure of one thing: Only a miracle could put it out!

Just then, four mega-tread tires skidded to a stop in the parking lot. This awesome fire-fighting vehicle was known as the Flame Racer — the creation of Tonka Joe, the world's greatest mechanic. No problem was too big for Tonka Joe.

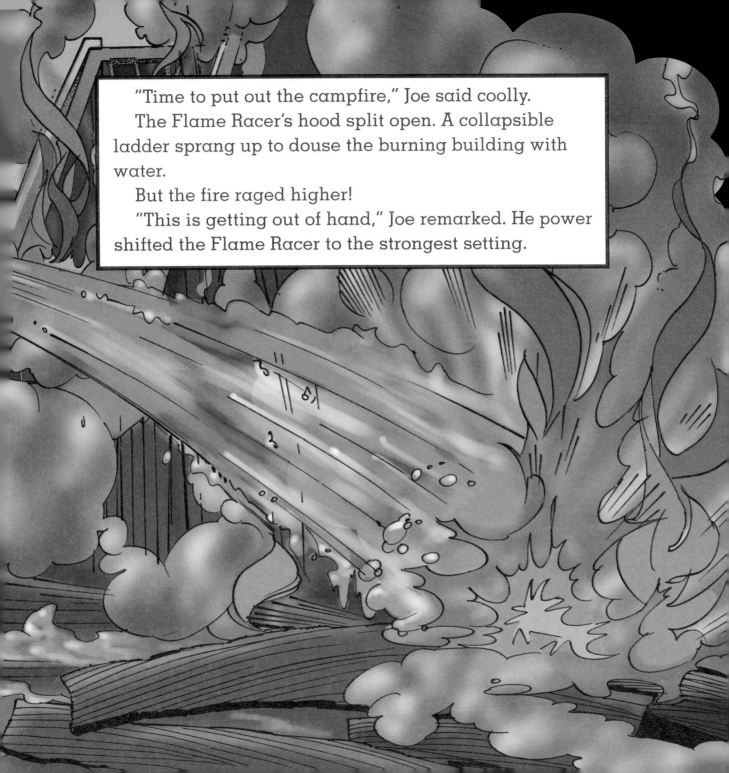

"Time to put out the campfire," Joe said coolly.

The Flame Racer's hood split open. A collapsible ladder sprang up to douse the burning building with water.

But the fire raged higher!

"This is getting out of hand," Joe remarked. He power shifted the Flame Racer to the strongest setting.

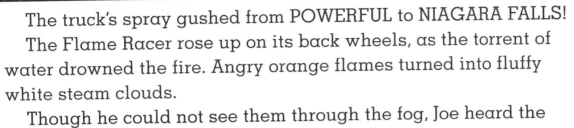

The truck's spray gushed from POWERFUL to NIAGARA FALLS! The Flame Racer rose up on its back wheels, as the torrent of water drowned the fire. Angry orange flames turned into fluffy white steam clouds.

Though he could not see them through the fog, Joe heard the firemen cheer. Joe cheered, too.

"It worked, J.J., the fire is dying down!" Joe told his teenage niece over the Flame Racer's communicator. J. J. was a whiz with computers. And Joe counted on her to help him run the workshop where he built special trucks for special jobs like fighting fires.

Then Joe suddenly remembered he was supposed to meet J.J.'s younger cousin, Stevie, at the bus stop. "I'm so late! This is a disaster!" he cried. He dreaded disappointing his nephew.

"Your Flame Racer *is* an emergency vehicle," J.J. reminded him.

Stevie waited at the bus stop, looking at a toy. He liked figuring out how things worked, and wondered if Uncle Joe would let him help in the workshop. But where *was* Uncle Joe, anyway? Stevie looked up at the clock, then up and down the street.

Meanwhile, Joe raced across town, careening wildly through a blur of traffic, bouncing down a hill of stairs, until . . .

Oh, no! The Flame Racer was stuck at a railroad crossing! Tonka Joe couldn't wait for the train to pass. He saw a ramp and . . . the Flame Racer jumped onto the train, switched into reverse just before slamming into the tunnel, then dropped to the ground, ready to race on!

A shadow fell over Stevie's toy. The little boy looked up into the tires of the biggest truck he'd ever seen.

The door swung open and his Uncle Joe leaned down and smiled. "Welcome to Minnetonka," he said.

"You were late," Stevie scolded.
"I'm sorry," Joe apologized. "There was a little traffic."
Stevie thought a summer in Minnetonka might be boring.
But Uncle Joe said, "Lots of interesting things happen here."

"Mega-awesome!" Stevie gasped when he saw Joe's amazing workshop. The place was as big as an airplane hangar and full of every kind of tool, truck, and tire.

"Hop on!" Joe said.

Suddenly, Stevie was swinging across the vast concrete floor. Ahead was a shiny new vehicle! Stevie had never seen anything so spectacular. Joe called his awesome creation the Path Cutter.

"I'm not sure what it does yet," the great mechanic confessed.

Stevie grinned. "I've got lots of ideas!" Maybe this summer wouldn't be so boring after all! Stevie's thoughts were interrupted by J.J.'s voice.

"There's an avalanche heading straight for Minnetonka!" J.J. announced over the workshop's computer.

Joe grabbed his snow-tool belt from the rack, the one he wore when he drove the Blizzard Rig.

"Can I come with you?" Stevie asked.

J.J. climbed into the souped-up snowplow, too.

Soon, Stevie stared at a giant wall of snow crashing toward the truck like a white tidal wave. "Are you sure one truck can handle that?"

"This isn't just any truck," J.J. said. "The Blizzard Rig is one of our Uncle Joe's trucks."

Joe smiled. "It's just a little snow."

The avalanche was more than just a little snow.
This was part blizzard, part Ice Age!
Joe power shifted his mighty machine . . .

and the Blizzard Rig's steel blade expanded from plow to PLOW!!! The bright blade pushed a heap of snow a hundred times its size! Tonka Joe grinned. His truck had tamed a mountain!

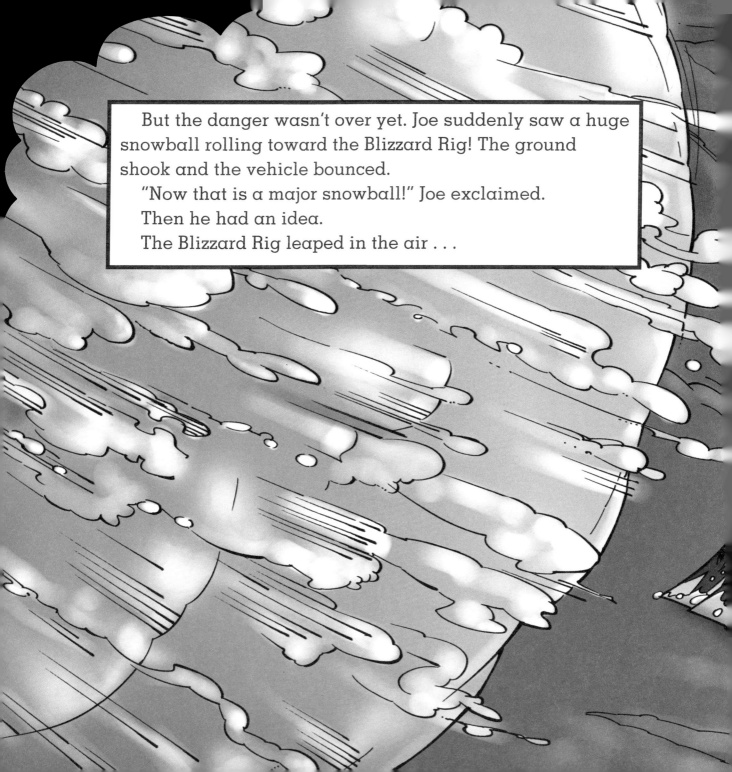

But the danger wasn't over yet. Joe suddenly saw a huge snowball rolling toward the Blizzard Rig! The ground shook and the vehicle bounced.

"Now that is a major snowball!" Joe exclaimed.

Then he had an idea.

The Blizzard Rig leaped in the air . . .

and rammed into the overgrown snowball! The ball shattered into delicate flakes that drifted down around the truck as gently as cherry blossoms in the spring.

J.J. hoped the wild leap hadn't damaged the Blizzard Rig.

"Not a scratch on her," Joe replied.

Soon, Joe, J.J., and Stevie were back at the mega-shop, working on the Path Cutter.

Stevie quickly handed his uncle the torque wrench he needed. Joe said, "I guess knowing tools runs in the family."

Stevie smiled. Maybe this visit would be the best ever. And maybe someday he would build trucks as cool as the Blizzard Rig and as hot as the Flame Racer!